Jonathan Swift
GULLIVER'S TRAVELS

essay by
Gregory Feeley

Gulliver's Travels

art by Lillian Chestney
adaption by Dan Kushner
cover by Bo Hampton

For Classics Illustrated Study Guides
computer recoloring by Colorpillar
editor: Madeleine Robins
assistant editor: Gregg Sanderson
design: Scott Friedlander

Classics Illustrated: Gulliver's Travels © Twin Circle Publishing Co.,
a division of Frawley Enterprises; licensed to First Classics, Inc.
All new material and compilation © 1997 by Acclaim Books, Inc.

Dale-Chall R.L.: 6.85

ISBN 1-57840-062-7

Classics Illustrated® is a registered trademark of the Frawley Corporation.

Acclaim Books, New York, NY
Printed in the United States

STUDY GUIDE

EIGHT HUNDRED YARDS ACROSS THE WATER LIES BLEFUSCU. ITS FLEET, CONSISTING OF FIFTY MEN-OF-WAR, LIES AT ANCHOR, READY FOR THE NEXT DAY'S INVASION.

WADING AND SWIMMING, GULLIVER REACHES THE ENEMY VESSELS.

HE TIES A ROPE TO EACH HOOK, THEN PLACES A HOOK IN THE HOLE AT THE PROW OF EACH SHIP.

UNDISTURBED BY A HAIL OF ARROWS FROM THE SHORE, GULLIVER JOINS THE ROPES TOGETHER AND HEADS BACK TOWARD LILLIPUT, TAKING THE ENTIRE BLEFUSCU FLEET WITH HIM...

YOUR MAJESTY, THESE SHIPS ARE NOW YOURS.

YOU HAVE SAVED OUR COUNTRY. NO HONOR IS TOO GREAT FOR YOU.

IF I DON'T DO SOMETHING, THIS GULLIVER WILL REPLACE ME AS ADMIRAL.

BACK IN BLEFUSCU, CAPTURE OF THE GREAT FLEET HAS STUNNED THE ENEMY. THE KING HASTILY CALLS A WAR COUNCIL.

THIS GIANT IS TOO MUCH FOR US. WE MUST MAKE PEACE WITH LILLIPUT.

THE KING OF BLEFUSCU COMES TO LILLIPUT TO SEEK PEACE TERMS.

BLEFUSCU WILL NEVER MAKE WAR ON YOUR NATION AGAIN.

GOOD! LET US LIVE IN PEACE!

THE KING LEAVES LILLIPUT AFTER A VISIT TO THE GREAT GULLIVER, WHOM HE HAS INVITED TO BE HIS GUEST IN BLEFUSCU... BUT GULLIVER REMAINS IN LILLIPUT, HOPING THAT HIS GREAT SIZE AND STRENGTH WILL AGAIN BE OF SERVICE TO THE LITTLE PEOPLE THERE.

SECRETLY, BOLGOLAM PREPARES FOR THE ASSAULT.

BUT BEFORE LAUNCHING THE TREACHEROUS ATTACK, HE INTENDS TO MAKE SURE THAT GULLIVER WILL BE UNABLE TO INTERFERE. HE PLANS TO CONVINCE THE EMPEROR THAT GULLIVER MUST BE DONE AWAY WITH. A HENCHMAN BRINGS HIM THE NEWS THAT HE HAS BEEN WAITING FOR...

YOUR CHANCE HAS COME! I HAVE JUST LEARNED THAT THE BLEFUSCU AMBASSADOR WILL VISIT GULLIVER TONIGHT!

GOOD! I WILL BE THERE MYSELF TO WATCH.

THAT NIGHT...

HERE COMES THE AMBASSADOR! WE'LL WATCH THROUGH THE WINDOW. CAREFUL, NOW...

GULLIVER RECEIVES THE AMBASSADOR CORDIALLY, UNAWARE THAT HIS EVERY MOVE IS BEING WATCHED BY THE TREACHEROUS, SPYING PAIR WHO SEEK HIS DOOM.

THE AMBASSADOR BECOMES ATTRACTED BY GULLIVER'S WATCH AND GULLIVER IN FRIENDLY SPIRIT OFFERS IT TO HIM FOR A SOUVENIR. THE AMBASSADOR, WISHING TO RETURN THE TOKEN OF FRIENDSHIP, PROMISES TO BRING GULLIVER SOME GOLD COINS ON THE FOLLOWING NIGHT... AS A SOUVENIR OF BLEFUSCU.

THAT IS ALL BOLGOLAM NEEDS TO HEAR... HURRYING TO THE EMPEROR, HE REPORTS THAT GULLIVER IS SELLING OUT MILITARY SECRETS TO BLEFUSCU FOR GOLD. "I CAN'T BELIEVE IT!" EXCLAIMS THE EMPEROR. "I WILL SHOW YOU PROOF," SMILES BOLGOLAM, "TOMORROW NIGHT."

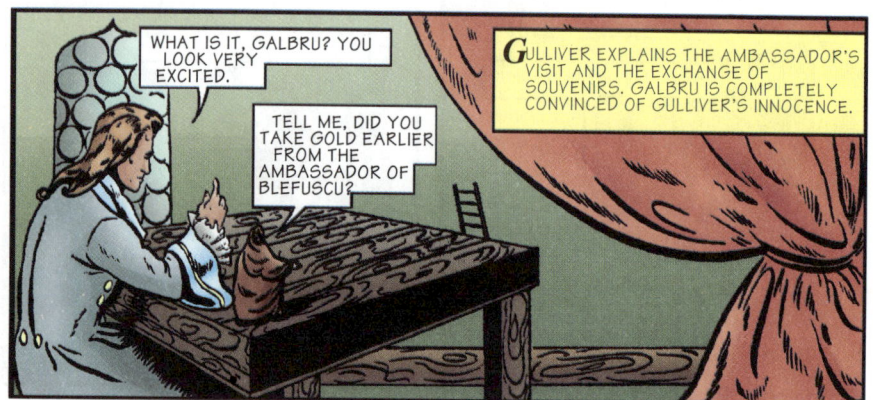

GULLIVER'S TRAVELS
JONATHAN SWIFT

Jonathan Swift's *Gulliver's Travels* is one of the world's best-known and most beloved tales, a novel that has been enjoyed by readers of all ages for more than two hundred years. Written as a sharp, sometimes bitter satire of the religious and political practices of the 1720s, Swift's novel can also be read as an entertaining series of adventures—first in the tiny kingdom of Lilliput, then later among the giants of Brobdingnag and a succession of even stranger lands.

One mark of a literary classic is how well it holds up to adaptation—to retelling by other artists in their own manner, for their own era. *Gulliver's Travels* has been adapted for film, TV, and comic-book versions (the first graphic adaptation of the story was in the 1850s!). The Classics Illustrated adaptation of *Gulliver's Travels* gives full scope to Lemuel Gulliver's adventures (and mishaps) in the kingdom of Lilliput. But to fully appreciate Swift's satiric genius the reader must go to the book itself. And although the novel is extremely easy to read—Swift read passages aloud to his servants, to make sure that every sentence was clear and straightforward—much of its complexity requires some knowledge of Swift's own life and the tumultuous times he lived in.

The Author

Jonathan Swift, the greatest satirist in the English language, was born on November 30, 1667, in Dublin, Ireland, the son of British parents whose families had settled in Ireland as prosperous middle-class professionals. Ireland was a poor country, dominated (and often ill-treated) by its English masters, and Swift's father, who had a position of steward at the King's Inns (the establishment where law students lived) could reasonably expect a prosperous life for his wife and young family. However, he died suddenly in early 1667, leaving his wife pregnant with their second child. Young Jonathan was born fatherless and into financially insecure circumstances.

Swift and his sister Jane grew up with the financial assistance of an uncle, who sent Jonathan to good schools but was emotionally distant. Swift seemed to feel keenly the lack of a father figure, and grew up emotionally insecure.

At the age of six he was sent to Kilkenny School, then the finest school in Ireland, and entered Trinity College at the age of fourteen. Trinity was the finest university in Ireland, but Swift felt that his uncle had given him "the education of a dog," by which he evidently meant that as the child of English parents, who was Irish only by the accident of birth, Oxford and Cambridge would have been more appropriate.

Swift graduated four years later, but evidently found his college years unhappy and demeaning; he was so distressed by what he called "the ill-treatment of his nearest relatives" (meaning his mother and sister) by his father's family that he neglected his studies. In his autobiography, he expressed his mortification that he graduated only *speciali gratia* ("by special favor"). The term refers to a special permission for a deserving student (who had failed to conform to academic in some trivial way) to be granted a degree; Swift's chagrin over what he regarded as a "discreditable mark" against his name was unfounded.

Swift continued to study for his Master's degree until early 1689, when the political discord then wracking the kingdom compelled him to move to England for greater safety. In 1688 the "Glorious Revolution" had deposed the Catholic James II from the British throne and installed his Protestant daughter Mary in her place. The conflict between the "Whigs" (who strongly opposed Catholicism) and the "Tories" (who supported the divine rights of kings, even Catholic kings) caused considerable unrest in Catholic Ireland, especially when James fled there and installed his own Parliament in Dublin. The British, Protestant, Swift decided to join his mother, who was living with relatives in England.

His mother's family connections allowed Swift to be introduced to Court society, like any young (British) gentleman. Swift spent ten years as a secretary to his kinsman Sir William Temple, and learned more during this period (Sir William had an excellent library) than he had at Trinity. Sir William was a Whig, and Swift, who regarded his benefactor as more a father to him than his uncle had been, became a Whig, too.

Swift returned briefly to Ireland, where he was ordained a priest of the Anglican Church. He remained a member of Sir William's household, however, and while there he began to write poems and satires. Although Swift continued to write poetry throughout his life, it was his satires that proved the wellspring of his creative genius. In "The Battle of the Books," Swift wrote a mock epic tale of a battle between ancient and modern books, with the ancient ones (and, by implication, classical values generally) coming out the winner. *A Tale of a Tub*, one of Swift's greatest works, is a satiric allegory—a tale in which the characters represent institutions (or emotions, or belief systems, or other people) that are the author's actual subject. The *Tale* tells the story of three brothers: Peter (Catholicism), Martin (the established Protestantism of Luther and the Anglican Church), and Jack (the Calvinist dissenters), whose Father (Christ) leaves each of them a will (the New Testament) and a new coat (the Church). Swift's account of how the brothers treat their coats and get along with each other cunningly duplicates the history of Christianity. The story's conclusion: that only Martin took care of his coat, while Peter covered his with so much embroidery, fringe, and lace that "there was hardly a thread of the original coat to be seen," while Jack so tears at his coat that he reduces it to tatters. Readers had no problem concluding that Swift's sympathies lay entirely with the Church of England.

A Tale of a Tub was a great success, and Jonathan Swift became a famous man. He took part in public affairs, wrote political pamphlets, and became friends with the great men of his time, including the poet Alexander Pope and the playwright John Gay (author of *The Beggar's Opera*). Although he enjoyed this celebrity, Swift changed parties when the Whigs began to make political concessions to the Dissenters, whom he regarded as a much greater threat than the Catholics. This daring move would have a high price.

Swift dreamed of being made a bishop, but his ambitions were dashed in 1713 when he was given the deanery of St. Patrick's Cathedral in Dublin, rather than one of the English deaneries then vacant. There were reports that Queen Anne had regarded *A Tale of a Tub* as irreligious, but a likelier reason was Swift's Irish birth: however much Swift considered himself an Englishman, and however much he shared the English scorn for Ireland, to the English court he was essentially Irish himself.

Swift took up his position—a lifelong appointment—in Dublin, to which he felt he had been sent like "a poisoned rat to die in a hole." He regarded it as a most bitter exile: Ireland was mostly Catholic, and the Protestant minority was more likely to be Dissident than Anglican. Not only was Swift exiled among people he despised, they were also largely his enemies. A year later Queen Anne died and George I, who had been supported by the Whigs, became King. George left the government in control of his Whig ministers, and any chance of Swift resurrecting his political career was ended.

For some years Swift withdrew from the public eye, feeling that life in "Wretched Dublin in miserable Ireland" was no life at all. Gradually, however, he roused himself, and became an active champion of the Irish people, whose unjust treatment by the English moved him to indignant action. "A Modest Proposal," an essay that sardonically proposed that poor Irish families could best reduce their poverty by selling their babies to be eaten by paying Englishman, is one of the most ferocious satires ever written. "The Drapier's Letters," a series of letters supposedly written by a simple Dublin linen-maker, attacked a British scheme to flood Ireland with devalued currency. Swift's relentless opposition to the corrupt plan (an open secret in Dublin) eventually brought a price upon his head—the British government offered a reward of £300 for the drapier's identity—but nobody turned him in. In the end, Swift prevailed in his single-handed war against the British, and the plan to introduce the debased currency was abandoned. Swift was hailed as an Irish national hero.

But the most famous work of Swift's later years—indeed of his entire life—was the one published in 1726 as *Travels into Several Remote Locations of the World, by Lemuel Gulliver*. Issued with no other byline, as though it were indeed the non-fiction account it pretended to be, the book was an immediate and immense success. Wrote Pope and Gay in a joint letter to Swift: "From the highest to the lowest it is universally read, from the cabinet council to the nursery." Swift had feared that its satire might cause the book to be prosecuted, and had told Pope that publication would have to wait until "a printer shall be found brave enough to venture his ears" (i.e., risk having his ears cut off for publishing a subversive work), so kept his name off it. But everyone recognized the work as his, and everyone was entranced by it. Swift once told Pope that he intended the work to "vex the world rather than divert it," but the world was delighted.

Travels into Several Remote Locations of the World was immediately reprinted and translated in several European languages, and its title was almost immediately changed to *Gulliver's Travels*. Readers debated its meaning; one publisher brought out a "key" purporting to explain the various allegories and hidden references. The Duchess of Marlborough, whom Swift had once attacked, was said to be "in raptures at it; she says she can dream about nothing else since she read it." A respectable bishop, on the other hand, claimed that the book was "full of improbable lies, and for his part, he hardly believed a word of it."

Swift never wrote another full-length book, but he continued to write satirical and political essays through the 1730s. In 1739 Dublin held a great celebration in honor of Swift's seventy-second birthday, confirming his status as Ireland's foremost citizen. Swift published his last major work in that year, the sardonic yet touching poem, "Verses on the Death of Dr. Swift." Despite the prediction, Swift died only in 1745, at the age of seventy-eight.

The Plot

PART ONE: THE VOYAGE TO LILLIPUT

Lemuel Gulliver, an English physician, finds that he can't support his wife and family through his medical practice in London, and takes a position as a ship's surgeon on the *Antelope*. On one of the ship's voyages in the East Indies, the ship is wrecked in a terrible storm, and Gulliver escapes with five crew members on a life boat. A wave upsets the craft, and Gulliver swims until he reaches land. He crawls up onto the beach and falls asleep, exhausted.

When he wakes, he can't move: his arms, legs, and hair have been tied to the ground. He can't turn his head to see what has happened to him, but he hears a strange noise around him, and feels some creature moving up his left leg and onto his chest. To his astonishment, he sees a tiny man less than six inches tall looking at him.

The man carries a tiny bow and arrow, and Gulliver feels more tiny men moving over his body. He shouts in alarm, and they scatter. They soon return, however, and one of them

FOR A MOMENT HE IS STUNNED, THEN HE SHOUTS... AND IN TERROR THE LILLIPUTIANS SCURRY AWAY.

addresses Gulliver in an unfamiliar language. When the bewildered castaway begins to pull his hand free, he feels more than a hundred arrows strike his hand and face. There is an army of tiny men surrounding him.

Stories of travelers who enter a strange land and discover fantastical beings are as old as Western literature, but Swift's account of Gulliver's first contact with the Lilliputians is remarkable in several respects. Swift describes the "human creature" as not quite six inches high, and he maintains that one-to-twelve ratio. This may be the first example in English literature of a fantastic idea carried out with such attention to detail. (Swift also notes that the Lilliputians, with their tiny vocal chords, have high-pitched voices.) The fact that the Lilliputians speak their own language, as incomprehensible to Gulliver as his is to them, is another detail that nobody had thought of before. (The foreigners in Shakespeare's *The Winter's Tale* and the fairies in *A Midsummer Night's Dream* all speak English.)

Gulliver decides to lie still, and the Lilliputians stop firing upon him. A well-dressed Lilliputian, whom Gulliver takes to be "a Person of Quality" (that is, a gentleman or aristocrat), makes a long speech at him, after which Gulliver indicates by gestures that his intentions are peaceful. Gulliver also makes clear that he's extremely hungry, and he is brought some food. After finishing the meal (entire cuts of meat, loaves of bread no larger than musket balls, and several tiny Lilliputian barrels of wine), Gulliver is able to roll far enough onto his side to relieve himself, which causes the Lilliputians close to him to scatter out of the way.

This attention to bodily functions (which Swift returns to later) is unusual in 18th-century fiction. The reason is not prudishness—English society during the reign of Queen Anne was considerably more open about such matters than the Victorians of a century later. But the novel was still a new form, and earlier writers hadn't felt it necessary to pay much attention to physical detail. Daniel Defoe's *Robinson Crusoe* (1719)—the tale of how a shipwrecked man creates a home for himself out of the resources available to him—was unusually detailed: it was realistic, like a memoir (which, indeed, Defoe at first pretended it was) rather than fanciful like a fable. Although Swift's novel was fabulous in its adventures, he wrote about them with scrupulous realism and detail.

Gulliver falls asleep soon after finishing his meal—he later learns that the wine had been drugged—and while he slumbers the Lilliputians lift his body with eighty long poles rigged with ropes and pulleys, and place it on a great wagon ("a Frame of Wood raised three inches from the Ground, about seven Feet long and four wide, moving upon twenty two Wheels"). It takes fifteen hundred horses to pull him the half mile to the city.

Gulliver is taken to an abandoned

temple, which has an entrance large enough for him to crawl inside. Thousands of people come to stare at him, while Lilliputian engineers shackle his left leg with ninety-one tiny chains ("like those that hang to a Lady's Watch in Europe"). When they are certain that he can't break loose, they untie the bonds that hold Gulliver to the wagon, and he crawls miserably into the temple to spend the night.

The next morning the Emperor of Lilliput arrives and looks at Gulliver. Gulliver makes a good impression upon his Majesty, who orders a bed and a new suit of clothes to be made for him, and arranges for enough bread, meat and wine to be brought to him every day to keep him fed. Over a period of weeks Gulliver learns the language of the Lilliputians, and implores the Emperor to grant him his freedom. Eventually the Emperor grants him this, on condition that Gulliver swear to obey certain regulations, including a promise never to enter the capital city without giving two hours' notice.

Gulliver becomes a member of the royal court, and observes its various customs and intrigues. This allows Swift to present a complex satire of British politics during the reign of Queen Anne. (See "Leaping and Creeping: Life in the Lilliputian Court," below.) Gulliver, who is careful to offend no one, enjoys the confidence of Reldresal, the Principal Secretary of Private Affairs, but has become—"without any Provocation," he insists—the enemy of Skyresh Bolgolam, the High Admiral. Since Lilliput is locked in a long struggle with the neighboring empire of Blefuscu and fears an imminent invasion, court politics is an especially treacherous business, which the naive and clumsy Gulliver can scarcely follow.

THE EMPEROR'S ADMIRATION OF GULLIVER WORRIES ADMIRAL BOLGOLAM, WHO HAS GAINED ROYAL FAVOR FOR HIMSELF AND DREAMS OF WINNING GREAT POWER.

I MUST NOT LET THIS MONSTER GET IN MY WAY.

While Gulliver's great size makes him an inept courtier, it proves to have other advantages. When the Blefuscuns assemble a great fleet of ships and prepare to cross the channel separating the two empires, Gulliver is able to rout the invasion single-handedly. He swims across the channel, then wades up to the Blefuscu fleet as it rides at anchor in the harbor, preparing to sail with the first fair wind. While the Blefuscu archers fire thousands of arrows at him, Gulliver cuts the cables that fasten the anchors, loops a chain through the prows of the boats, and tows the entire fleet back to Lilliput.

The emperor is so delighted with Gulliver that he makes him a *Nardac*—"the highest Title of honour" in Lilliput. But when the emperor orders Gulliver to return to Blefuscu and bring all of its ships to Lilliput, Gulliver realizes that "so unmeasurable is the Ambition of Princes, that he seemed to think of nothing less than reducing the whole Empire of

Blefuscu into a Province," and so become, in his imagination, "sole Monarch of the whole World." Gulliver attempts to explain that this would be a bad idea, but his arguments—based on "Policy" as well as "Justice"—do not persuade his Imperial Majesty, and Gulliver ends by flatly refusing to be "an Instrument of bringing a free and brave People into Slavery."

The Lilliputian emperor never forgives Gulliver, and soon a plot is hatched against him. Gulliver observes: "Of so little weight are the greatest Services to Princes, when put into the Balance with a Refusal to gratify their Passions."

When a delegation from Blefuscu comes to make peace with Lilliput, Gulliver speaks in a friendly manner to them. Although this is proper behavior, the Lilliputian emperor behaves coldly to Gulliver afterward, and he later learns that his enemies have suggested to his Majesty that Gulliver may be suspect in his sympathies. He concludes bitterly: "And this was the first time I began to conceive some perfect Idea of Courts and Ministers."

Swift then follows this scene—which began with adventure, and ended in disillusioned reflection—with a very different one. Not long after Gulliver captures the Blefuscun fleet, he is awaked one night by a crowd outside his door. The Imperial Palace is on fire, and the Queen's apartments are being destroyed. The Lilliputians provide Gulliver with buckets of water to throw on the fire, but the buckets are "about the Size of a large Thimble," and do little good. "The Case seemed wholly desperate and deplorable; and this magnificent Palace would have infallibly been burnt to the ground," Gulliver reports, "if, by a Presence of Mind unusual to me, I had not suddenly thought of an Expedient." In a scene that does not often make it into modern versions of the story, Gulliver empties his bladder onto the fire, which succeeds in putting it out. Though the palace is saved, Gulliver worries about how his act shall be received, for (as he judiciously puts it): "Although I had done a very eminent Piece of Service, yet I could not tell how his Majesty might resent the Manner in which I had performed it." Indeed, the Queen is so offended by his actions that she swears revenge for this affront.

After this, things go downhill fast for Gulliver. He dines with his Majesty, shows off by eating more than usual, and thus gives the royal Treasurer, one of his enemies, the chance to remind the emperor how much it cost to feed him. Worse, Gulliver allows himself to be caught up in a ridiculous Court scandal. He's quick to supply the details:

> I am here obliged to vindicate the Reputation of an excellent Lady, who was an innocent Sufferer upon my Account. The Treasurer took a Fancy to be jealous of his Wife, from the Malice of some evil Tongues, who informed him that her Grace had taken a violent Affection for my Person; and the Court-Scandal ran for

some Time that she had once came privately to my Lodging. This I solemnly declare to be a most infamous Falsehood, without any Grounds, farther than that her Grace was pleased to treat me with all innocent Marks of Freedom and Friendship. I own she came often to my House, but always publickly, nor ever without three more in the Coach, who were usually her Sister, and young Daughter, and some particular Acquaintance . . .

Gulliver has no sense of the ridiculousness of these charges; he has (literally) lost perspective, and forgotten the gross difference in size between himself and the Lilliputians. His indignation at the gossip surrounding the Treasurer's wife doesn't entirely mask how flattered he is at being treated like a member of the Court, even if only because he's the subject of malicious rumors.

In addition, Gulliver has allowed his own vanity to blind him, as his concluding protest shows:

I should not have dwelt so long upon this Particular if it had not been a Point wherein the Reputation of a great Lady is so nearly concerned, to say nothing of my own; although I had the Honour to be a Nardac, which the Treasurer himself is not; for all the World knows he is only a Clumglum, a Title inferior by one degree . . .

Gulliver's honors have gone to his head, to the extent that he doesn't realize that he's in danger of losing it. It's not until one of his friends at Court comes privately to Gulliver and warns him that he's being charged with treason that he realizes the extent of his danger.

Gulliver's enemies have prepared numerous Articles of Impeachment against him, charging him with Blefuscan sympathies, with refusing to destroy the entire Blefuscan navy and reduce that nation to a Lilliputian province, and even with putting out the fire in the royal Palace!

Gulliver's enemies had urged that the emperor put him to death, but the emperor decides that it would be enough to put out both of Gulliver's eyes. It is, Gulliver's friend tells him, expected that Gulliver will "gratefully and humbly" submit to this sentence,

which shows the emperor's kindness and leniency. The horrified Gulliver reflects that "I must confess, having never been designed for a Courtier, either by my Birth or Education, I was so ill a Judge of Things, that I could not discover the Lenity and Favour of this Sentence; but conceived it (perhaps erroneously) rather to be rigorous than gentle." This blackly humorous sentence suggests that the petty vanity and fatuousness of the simple (and easily impressed) Lemuel Gulliver is nothing compared to the viciousness and pettiness of Court ministers and their kings, who proclaim their kindness and leniency just when they are being most vicious, ungrateful, and unjust.

Gulliver considers defending himself in court, but realizes that he can't rely on the justice of judges. He briefly thinks of attacking the palace, which he could easily destroy by hurling stones at it; but "I soon rejected that Project with Horror, by remembering the Oath I had made to the Emperor, the Favours I received from him, and the high Title of *Nardac* he conferred upon me. Neither had I so soon learned the Gratitude of Courtiers, to persuade myself that his Majesty's *present Severities acquitted me of all past Obligations*." It's a complex and poignant thought, beginning with Gulliver's hurt feelings (he still mourns the loss of royal favor he had so valued), then moving to an appreciation that a legitimate grievance does not cancel all obligations, which he frames in the form of a bitterly ironic remark about "the gratitude of courtiers."

Gulliver promptly flees Lilliput for Blefuscu, whose own emperor had previously invited him to make a visit. He says nothing about his "disgrace" in Lilliput, and is welcomed by the Blefuscun people, who know that he interceded on their behalf when the emperor of Lilliput wanted them enslaved. When the emperor of Lilliput sends a letter to Blefuscu ordering them to send back Gulliver "bound hand and foot," the Blefuscun emperor is able to claim, with a show of regret, that such a thing is physically impossible. In private, he offers Gulliver his royal protection if Gulliver agrees to continue in his service. "Although I believed him sincere," reports Gulliver, "yet I resolved never more to put any Confidence in Princes or Ministers." Gulliver has painfully learned that the honored and powerful aren't necessarily trustworthy.

When a boat from a European ship washes up on the shore of Blefuscu, Gulliver seizes the opportunity to return to home. With the emperor of Blefuscu's approval, he repairs the boat and outfits it for travel. Taking with him a number of cows and sheep, which he hopes to breed once he returns to England, Gulliver sets sail, and in a few days is picked up by an English ship. No one believes his story of the tiny empires of Lilliput and Blefuscu until he produces some of the cattle and sheep.

When he returns to England, Gulliver makes his fortune by exhibiting his cattle, and later selling them. His voyage has indeed made him a wealthy man, although not in the way he could ever have expected.

PART TWO: A VOYAGE TO BROBDINGNAG

Two months after returning to England, Gulliver sets out on another sea voyage, for "my insatiable desire of seeing foreign countries would suffer me to continue no longer." This time he's shipwrecked in Brobdingnag, a country of giants. Brobdingnagians are twelve times the height of a

Leaping and Creeping: Life in the Lilliputian Court

Jonathan Swift's account of the laws and customs in Lilliput, especially in the royal Court, are among his harshest and most pointed satires. Some of it can't be understood except through familiarity with the political issues of Swift's day; others are timeless and universal.

As Gulliver soon discovers, the Lilliputian court is divided into two factions, the "Tramecksan" and the "Slamecksan," who can be distinguished by whether they wear high or low heels on their shoes. "The Animosities between these two Parties run so high," a minister tells Gulliver, "that they will neither eat nor drink, nor talk with each other." The minister adds that while his Majesty favors the Low-Heels, "We apprehend his Imperial Highness, the Heir to the Crown, to have some Tendency toward the High-Heels; at least we can plainly discover one of his Heels higher than the other; which gives him a Hobble in his Gait."

You don't need to know any English history to enjoy the humor in this, but Swift isn't just making fun of factionalism in general. The High- and the Low-Heels represent the Tories and the Whigs, and Swift is commenting on the fact that while George I had always favored the Whigs, his son, Prince George (in whom both parties were beginning to take an interest, as the aging George had begun to lose his health), was uncertain in his loyalties—hence, he could be said to wear one high heel and one low, and as a consequence be human, so they look to Gulliver the way he looked to the Lilliputians. While Gulliver was a threatening figure to the Lilliputians, the Brobdingnagians treat him like a pet.

Gulliver's tale of life in Brobdingnag has much of the charm and drama of his adventures in Lilliput; and children's versions of the novel often include this section as well. Gulliver finds life in Brobdingnag even more difficult than Lilliput had been: at one point he's attacked by wasps, whom he must fight off with his sword; at another he's picked up by a tame monkey, who holds him to her breast and attempts to nurse him. Swift again uses the social system of his invented country as a way of satirizing English society:

> *The learning of this People is very defective; consisting only in Morality, History, Poetry and Mathematicks; wherein they must be allowed to excel. But the last of these is wholly applied to what may be useful in Life; to the Improvement of Agriculture and all mechanical Arts; so that among us it would be little esteemed. And as to Ideas, Entities, Abstractions and Transcendentals, I could never drive the least Conception into their Heads.*
>
> *No Law of that Country must exceed in Words the Number of Letters in their Alphabet, which consists only of two and twenty. But indeed, few of them extend even to the Length. They are expressed in the most plain and simple Terms, wherein those People are not Mercurial enough to discover above one Interpretation. And to write a Comment upon any Law is a capital Crime.*

unable to walk straight.

The other, and even more long-standing, dispute in Lilliput rages between the Big-Endians and the Little-Endians, who disagree over what end of the shell one should break when eating an egg. Tradition long decreed that eggs were broken on the big end, but when the present emperor's grandfather once, as a little boy, cut his finger while doing so, "his father published an edict commanding all his Subjects, upon great Penalties, to break the smaller End of their Eggs." In the decades since, "there have been six Rebellions raised on that Account, wherein one Emperor lost his Life and another his Crown." Because the Big-Endian rebellions have been encouraged by Blefuscu, and the unsuccessful rebels have always found refuge there, the two empires have long been at war.

The conflict between the Big-Endians and the Little-Endians parallels the rise of Protestantism in England, a bloody struggle in which one English King lost his life (Charles II) and another his Crown (James II). Blefuscu obviously represents France, a Catholic kingdom that long supported English Catholics in their attempts to return their country to Catholic rule. The analogy is not exact—the English religious wars involved three factions, as Swift showed in *A Tale of A Tub*—but no contemporary reader of Swift's could be in any doubt as to what he was getting at.

No reader can mistake Swift's actual attitude toward these supposedly deplorable qualities, or toward the conventional Gulliver for failing to appreciate them.

Gulliver leaves Brobdingnag when the carrying case he's traveling in is grabbed by an eagle, who flies off with it. The box is dropped into the ocean, and after bobbing in the water for a few hours, it's picked up by a British ship. Gulliver is once more rescued by his own countrymen and returned to England.

PART THREE: A VOYAGE TO LAPUTA, BALNIBARBI, GLUBBDUBDRIB, LUGGNAG AND JAPAN

Part Three of *Gulliver's Travels*, "A Voyage to Laputa, Balnibarbi, Glubbdubdrib, Luggnagg, and Japan," and Part Four, "A Voyage to the Country of the Houyhnhnms," are rarely included in children's editions or dramatized versions of the novel, and most readers do not encounter them until they read the novel itself.

In his third voyage, Gulliver encounters the flying city of Laputa, whose citizens are so lost in abstracted thought that they must be followed by servants carrying sticks, who bop them gently on the head to return them to reality. The Laputans are a rather obvious satire of scientists of Swift's day, whose interest in pure science, mathematics, and music theory—that is, with theory rather than with application—Swift regarded with repugnance. Gulliver also visits the grand Academy of Lagado, where scientists

A Gulliver Glossary

Words from *Gulliver's Travels* That Have Entered the English Language

Big-Endians and Little-Endians—Partisans of a particularly vicious quarrel over some unimportant distinction.

Brobdingnagian—Outsized, of immense dimensions. A rather ornate term, not too often used.

Lilliputian—Startlingly small; perfectly shaped to a tiny scale. A much more commonly-used term.

Struldbrug—an immensely old, powerful individual, usually one of a group. Senator Strom Thurmond, who at 93 has represented South Carolina in the U.S. Senate since 1954, has been called a Struldbrug.

Yahoo—A loutish, anti-intellectual, or boorish individual.

---

labor on various mad projects, including a scheme to "extract Sun-Beams out of cucumbers." These experiments are based on actual research that scientists were then trying to carry out, which Swift read about in *Transactions of the Royal Society*, the science journal of his era.

Swift's scorn for such "happy proposals" is withering (he mentions scientists' conviction that "All the fruits of the Earth shall come to Maturity at whatever season we think fit to choose, and increase an Hundred Fold more than they do at present"), for he's as disdainful of impractical application as he is of theory *without* application. We may notice, however, that many of the Academy's proposals have in fact come to pass: farmers can now grow produce in winter, the "Green Revolution" has indeed increased yields a hundred fold, and gasohol is nothing but chemical energy (originally produced by the Sun) extracted from crops (although scientists use grain rather than cucumbers).

After Laputa, Gulliver travels to the nearby island of Glubbdubdrib, where magicians can summon up the spirits of the dead to explain the true facts of history; then to Luggnugg, where he meets the Struldbrugs, who live forever, and so "have their minds free and disengaged, without the Weight and Depression of Spirits caused by the continual Apprehension of Death." Rather than being liberated by eternal life, the Struldbrugs have degenerated into moral monstrosities, "opiniative, peevish, covetous, morose, vain, talkative, [and] incapable of Friendship." They have been spiritually deformed by their divorce from natural mortality.

From Luggnugg, Gulliver travels to Japan, where he is able to find a ship able to return him to Europe. Like the first two parts, this section ends with Gulliver restored to his family.

PART FOUR: A VOYAGE TO THE COUNTRY OF THE HOUYHNHNMS

In his fourth voyage, Gulliver encounters two of Swift's most famous creations: the brutish Yahoos, who embody humanity's enslavement to passion and unreason, and the Houyhnhnms, intelligent horses who represent the highest aspirations of human nature. Gulliver, who stands midway between the Houyhnhnms and the Yahoos in moral nature (just as he earlier stood midway between the Lilliputians and the Brobdingnagians in physical size), is more deeply affected by his encounter with these creatures than he was in his earlier voyages (from which he seemed to have learned rather little).

Although Gulliver refers to the Yahoos as "beasts," it's clear that they are human in form, though hairy and savage in appearance. The fact that the gentle Houyhnhnms (the word is apparently meant to be pronounced like a whinny) initially regard Gulliver as a strange-looking Yahoo is deeply mortifying to him, and he goes to great lengths to persuade them that he is nothing of the sort.

The Houyhnhnms are so superior to both human and Yahoo that Gulliver finds his own attempts to defend human society unpersuasive, and eventually becomes ashamed of his own humanity. He becomes as much like a Houyhnhnm as possible, and when he finally (against his will) is returned to England, he finds the practice and habits of humanity so repulsive that he can scarcely bear them. Gulliver explains that, with practice, he is able to bear the sight of an ordinary Englishman—"a lawyer, a pickpocket, a colonel, a fool, a lord, a gamester, a whoremonger," whoever— without feeling particular dismay, but when he sees such creatures exhibit pride, his disgust is intolerable. The novel ends with him making a plea to his readers that, "if they show any tincture of this absurd vice," to keep out of his sight!

A Book For All Ages

Gulliver's Travels has been enormously popular since its first publication, and this popularity has extended across every imaginable boundary: it appeals to children and to adults, to English readers and to foreigners, and has been the subject of numerous adaptations. The moment of Lemuel Gulliver's awakening to find himself tied to the ground and a tiny person standing on his chest is one of the most vivid and famous images in Western literature; even schoolchildren who haven't yet read the book immediately recognize it.

The story of Gulliver's encounter with the Lilliputians has transcended Swift's novel: it is, like Don Quixote attacking the windmill, Robinson Crusoe discovering a strange footprint, or Rip Van Winkle awakening to discover twenty years gone, a dramatic incident that seems so instantly comprehensible and universally applicable that it almost becomes a part of modern mythology. We can't imagine Jane Eyre living in any time but her own, but it's easy to imagine a Japanese Gulliver, a Gulliver who traveled with Ulysses, or a 25th-century Gulliver in space. The dislocations in scale that Gulliver encounters—he's first made to feel like a giant in a world that has suddenly shrunk, then he becomes a helpless imp in a world of giants—are utterly fantastical, but also familiar to us from the anxieties we experience in dreams.

Because the story of Gulliver's adventures in Lilliput is so universal in its appeal, it has been frequently adapted as a children's book. Most readers, in fact, first encounter the tale in one of these editions or else in a cartoon version (the 1940 Max Fleisher film is a good example). These volumes, however, are invariably expurgated: Gulliver's problems in taking care of basic bodily functions—to which Swift devotes careful and comic attention—are omitted, as is much of the story's satirical bite. Although Gulliver's second adventure among the Brobdingnagians is often included, the novel's third and fourth books are always excised. Lemuel Gulliver's adventure in the kingdom of tiny people (and sometimes its sequel in the land of the giants) is a story that children can enjoy, but the rest of Swift's complex, funny, and often troubling book is definitely for grownups only.

In fact, the reputation of *Gulliver's Travels* as a novel for adults has swung back and forth in the 270 years since its publication. Although it has never lost its appeal to children, *Gulliver's Travels* was widely considered a misanthropic and hateful novel in the 19th-century, when Swift's ferocious scorn for human folly seemed at odds with an expansive and optimistic era, and his earthy humor seemed unacceptably coarse. While Swift's contemporaries relished the book's political satire, the generations that followed—from the Enlightenment spirit of the latter 18th-century, to the gaiety of the Restoration era and the moralizing sentimentality of the Victorians—found Swift too harsh and pessimistic to swallow. In particular, the long decades of the Victorian era saw Swift portrayed as not merely a satirist and misanthrope, but a kind of moral monster, desecrating all that was good in human nature. One 1890s critic claimed that,

> *"It is a question not of morality but of decency, whether it is becoming to sit in the same room with the works of this divine... Are we to stand by and hear our nature libeled, and our purest affections beslimed, with-*

"Verses on the Death of Dr. Swift"

The Dean, if we believe Report,
Was never ill receiv'd at Court.
And for his Works in Verse and
    Prose,
I own my self no Judge of those:
Nor, can I tell what Criticks
    thought 'em;
But this I know, all People
    bought 'em;

As with a moral View design'd
To cure the vices of Mankind:
His Vein, ironically grave,
Exposed the Fool, and lash'd the
    Knave:
To steal a Hint was never known,
But what he writ, was all his own.

Jonathan Swift

out a word of protest?"

In other words, *Gulliver's Travels* (and presumably Swift's other satires) were not merely artistically excessive, but depraved.

But the 20th-century saw Swift viewed in a renewed light. Swift's irony, his sympathy for the wretched and the oppressed, and his radical skepticism about ability of religious and political institutions to improve human nature were more hospitably received by the Victorians' successors. A British critic, H.W. Nevinson, summed it up:

> *"It was not any spirit of hatred or cruelty but an intensely personal sympathy with suffering that tore his heart and kindled that furnace of indignation against the stupid, the hateful and the cruel to whom most suffering is due; and it was a furnace in which he himself was consumed. Writing while he was still a youth in* A Tale of a Tub*, he composed a terrible sentence, in which all his rage and pity and ironical bareness of style seem foretold: 'Last week,' he says, 'I saw a woman flayed, and you will hardly believe how much it altered her person for the worse.'"*

Today *A Tale of a Tub*, "A Modest Proposal," "Verses on the Death of Dr. Swift," and above all *Gulliver's Travels* are regarded as among the supreme works of satire in English, and Jonathan Swift as one of the geniuses of the 18th-century.

Study Questions

• Could *Gulliver's Travels* be considered science fiction, or is it more of a fantasy? Think in terms of what was known about science, and unexplored parts of the world, in the 1720s.

• If a reader of *Gulliver's Travels* did not know that its satire was directed at Swift's own contemporaries, what might he or she think about its applicability to our own times? Is this a valid way to approach a classic novel?

• Compare *Gulliver's Travels* with another novel of the same era, *Robinson Crusoe*. Both novels, although written for adults, have been popular for children as well. What do these superficially quite dissimilar novels have in common?

• In what way is Gulliver like a twentieth-century man in his reactions to the Lilliputians? In what way is he different? (One way to think about this question: How might a modern Gulliver have acted differently?)

About the Essayist:

Gregory Feeley is an essayist and science fiction writer whose reviews and essays have appeared in *The Atlantic Monthly*, *The Washington Post*, and New York *Newsday*. His novel *The Oxygen Barons* (Ace, 1990) is set on the Moon.